I0703403

Dancing On Sunbeams

by Lynne McSherry

For My Best Buddies

Imagine a place
You haven't been yet.
Grab your best buddy
A flashlight, a net...

Go to the edge of
Outrageous mile.
Jump off the edge
Get ready to smile.

If you were an orange
And I was a bee,
We'd fly to the ocean
And swim in the sea.

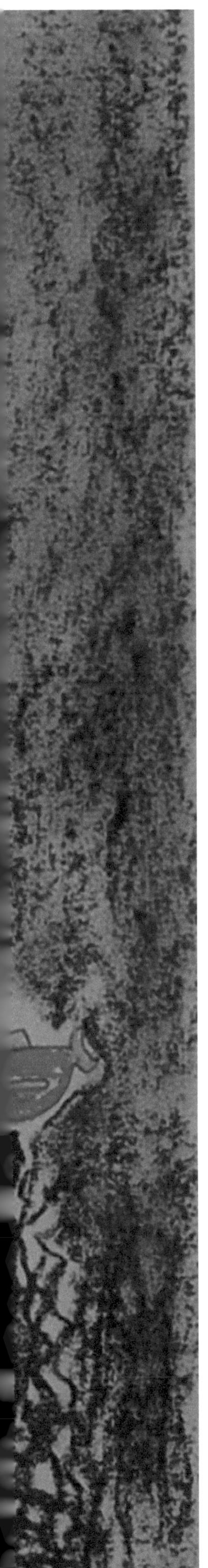

We'd dive through the water
And under the waves.
We'd visit some fish,
Explore deep, dark caves.

If you were a peacock,
I'd be your dragon.
We'd go on safari
To visit a lion.

Riding an elephant,
Sleeping with cheetahs,
Chasing giraffes
And laughing hyenas.

PLO

If you were a pilot
And I was your Ace,
We'd go on adventures,
Be astronauts in space.

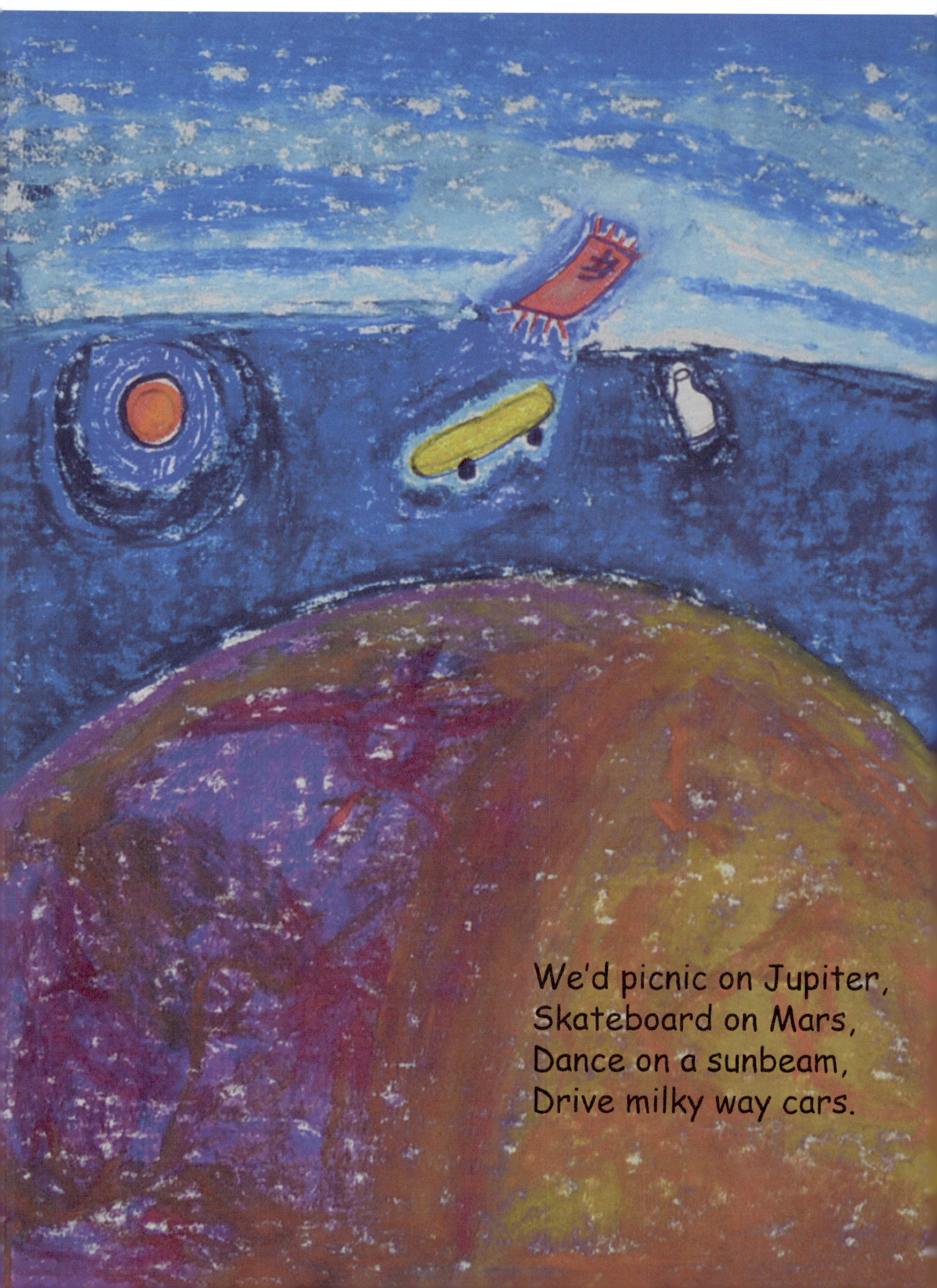
We'd picnic on Jupiter,
Skateboard on Mars,
Dance on a sunbeam,
Drive milky way cars.

If you were my pillow
And I was your teddy,
We'd snuggle up close,
Close our eyes and get ready...

Imagine a place
You haven't yet seen.
Grab your best buddy
And dream a great dream.